MR. MOORE'S MENAGERIE

A Bobby and Sonny Mystery

Anna Christian

DADIELTE PRODUCTION
MORENO VALLEY, CA

LCCN: 2019905099
ISBN -978-0-9981419-09

Published and distributed by
Dadielte Production
P.O. Box 1266
Moreno Valley, CA92556-1266

First Printing
Cover design by marcSierre' Design

For my family
Starla Rain, Maya, Hailey, Joseph Adedej and, Gabriel
And to Emily for sharing her story about bns

Chapter One

It's been a little over a year since Grandma came to live with us. This is a longest we've stayed in one place since Mama died. I'm feeling fine, like I finally belong somewhere. Not like before when we moved practically every month from place to place, not just in Harlem, but in the Bronx and Brooklyn, one ratty apartment after another. I know it was all my fault. Mama's dying through me for a loop. And I know I did a lot of bad things. She'd been sick a long time and when she died, it was left to me to raise my younger brothers Kevin and Kyle because Daddy worked nights.

I failed most of my classes in school, didn't stay in one place for long and couldn't make no friends that is until we moved here at 21 Bradhurst. Bobby and Sonny live in the building next door. Their families, Bobby's parents, Mr. and Mrs. Thompson, and Sonny's mother, Mrs. Henderson welcomed me and my family even though I'd caused them a lot of problems. Bobby, Sonny and me formed this club we call the Bradhurst Gumshoes like the Hardy Boys only we solve small problems around the neighborhood, like when somebody stole Bobby's bike and when somebody poured grease on the neighbors' clothes.

I like living here especially having Grandma with us. I don't have to look after my brothers as much. Daddy brought her up from Virginia where she was living with my Aunt Josephine and her family. Grandma said the house was crowded with all Josephine's kids underfoot and everybody treating her like she was helpless, making a fuss over her all the time whenever she tried to help out. She is a little hard of hearing but otherwise she seems fine. She said she was glad to come live with us.

"Maxine, what you all want for dinner? I'm about to make a pot of spaghetti and chopped meat," Grandma hollered from the kitchen.

"As soon as I finish my homework, I'll come in and help," I said.

"Tell Kevin to come here. I need to send him to the store to get some onions. Tell him to take Kyle with him."

Dragging them from "Superman," their favorite TV show, was like making them take a bath. They grumbled, "Why can't you go?"

"Cause I've got to finish my homework."

They must have run all the way to Sullivan's Market because they came rushing back.

"Sis, we got a new neighbor," said Kyle, all out of breath.

I looked up from the book I had to finish before class tomorrow. "So, what's so special about that? And besides he's not new. For your information he's been here at least two weeks."

I remembered when he moved in. It was the day Daddy said I could stay home from school because I was coming down with the flu. I was watching out the window when I saw this truck drive up and two men taking out boxes and bringing them into the building. I guess that must have been him. He was a small man, about a head shorter than Daddy with thick black hair peppered with gray. And he had a scraggly mustache. From what I could see, he had a nice looking face, pleasant like my math teacher Mr. Gray. He saw me looking down at him and winked. I ducked my head back in the window. Didn't want him to think I was spying on him.

"He was carrying a big cage. He had it covered with a cloth but then it slipped off and I could see an animal inside," said Kyle.

"Looked like one of those monitor lizards like I seen on Zoo Planet," said Kevin.

"Saw," I corrected him. "You must be joking. No animals except small dogs or cats are allowed in the building. Weren't you paying attention to the list of rules Daddy read to us when we first moved in?"

"Well, all I know is what I saw," said Kevin. "Right, little bro?" Kyle shook his head.

"Did you all get my onions?" Grandma shouted from the kitchen. "Bring them here so I can finish cooking dinner."

I turned back to the book I was reading, *Treasure Island*, but it wasn't holding my attention. Why would our new neighbor be bringing a wild animal into the small apartments in this building? Then I remembered that whenever I passed his door on my way up to the roof, I heard birds chirping. I thought it was on the television set.

I forgot all about it until I met up with Bobby and Sonny coming home from school a few days later. When I told them what my little brothers said, they had the same reaction. Why would somebody bring wild animals to a Harlem apartment?

"When did the neighbor move in?" Sonny asked.

"Not that long ago, maybe a few weeks, I think. His name is Mr. Moore I heard my Grandma tell my Daddy," I said.

"Come to think of it, I saw him walking down the street the other day," said Bobby. "He was carrying a big package. I never paid much attention, but I wondered what it could be." He grinned at us. "It may be a job for the Bradhurst Gumshoes."

"Why?" Sonny asked. "It doesn't seem to be our business."

"Why don't we go up to his apartment and introduce ourselves," said Bobby rubbing his hands together and smiling like he was ready for a tasty meal.

"I'm not too sure about that," I said. "What if he tells us to go away and mind our own business?"

"Yeah, I agree with Max. Anyway, I've got to go practice piano with Mrs. Griffin in a little while. You all go on, I'll see you later," Sonny said as he went into his building.

Just then we saw Mr. Moore coming down the street carrying a heavy cardboard box.

"How you kids doing?" He smiled as he struggled to open the outer door to the building. "Say, maybe you could give me a hand," he said to Bobby.

Bobby took the steps two at a time. Passing the package to Bobby, Mr. Moore opened the outer door. He took the box from Bobby and started up the stairs to his apartment. Bobby and I looked at each other as if to say we should follow him. We did. When Mr. Moore reached his door to unlock it, Bobby said, "Need any help?"

"Thank you, young man," he passed the box to Bobby and unlocked the door.

Once inside, he turned, took the box from Bobby and said, "Thanks for your help. I think I can manage it from here."

We watched him go inside and close the door behind him. "What do you think?" Bobby asked as we went downstairs to my apartment.

"What do I think about what?"

"About what Mr. Moore carried in that box. It wasn't that heavy and it seemed like something was moving inside."

"You're so dramatic," I said. "Probably some dishes, clothes, or stuff from his old apartment."

"I think we need to investigate this. There's something strange about him," Bobby said.

I sort of agreed with him but I wasn't in a hurry to get into another investigation. I'd finally managed to pull up my grades and though I didn't have to look after my brothers as much as before, I knew I should help Grandma around the apartment, probably. That would please Daddy. Bobby is always ready to go off on a new adventure getting us into trouble. Though it can be fun sometimes.

"Maybe we can talk to Sonny about this. If he says yes, I'm in," I said.

Sonny's the bright one. He thinks a lot and is just the opposite of Bobby, he's cautious. You wouldn't think a guy who couldn't see as much as you or me could be so smart, but Sonny is a genius. Even though he's blind, (he can see shadows and shapes), he can play the piano like nobody I've ever met, and he knows so much. I guess because his mother brings him a lot of books to read and encourages him to learn music.

Sometimes I wish I had a talent. I got the chance to sing at a church program last year and everyone said I had a good voice. So maybe I got some talent.

We talked it over with Sonny and he agreed we should find out as much about Mr. Moore as we could though I don't know what for. If he has wild animals in his apartment, maybe he works for a zoo and is keeping them for a while.

Sonny mapped out a plan. "First we have to find out where he works. If he's keeping strange animals in his apartment, maybe he works at a pet store or a zoo."

"But why would he need to bring animals home with him?" I asked.

"We got to get into his apartment and find out what animals he has," Bobby said.

They both looked at me. "Max, since he lives in your building, it may be easier for you to find out," said Sonny.

"I don't know about that," I said. I could see myself listening at his door and getting caught."

"I'll follow him," said Bobby. "I'll find out where he works and tail him."

"Suppose he works downtown. How are you gonna tail him on the subway when you hardly have money for a soda after school?" I asked.

"Well, I'll wait until he gets off from work and follow him from the subway."

"Tell you what, we'll give it a week and get together on Saturday to see what we got," said Sonny.

Chapter Two

All that week I waited on the stoop until I saw Mr. Moore leave for work which almost made me late for school. Then I went up to his door and put my ear to it. I heard birds chirping, heavy breathing, and some growling but I couldn't tell what it was. Strange. I even hid in the hallway when he came home to see if when he opened his door I might see inside. Nothing.

That Saturday, when we got together, Bobby said he didn't have nothing to report either. He said he waited at the subway for Mr. Moore and when he saw him, he wasn't carrying anything.

"I guess there's nothing to investigate," Sonny said. "Maybe it was sounds from the TV you heard."

"But why would the TV be on when he was away?" I asked.

Nobody had an answer so we put Mr. Moore's doings out of our minds. There were other more important things to concern Sonny.

"Mrs. Griffin wants to take me to visit a few music schools in Boston. She says I'm really talented and that she wants to see if I can get a scholarship to attend a school there."

"But the school term just started. Will your mother let you go?"

"It'll only be for a few weeks. Mrs. Griffin said she knows some important people and when she told them about me, they asked her to bring me for a visit. I'm not sure I want to go but my mother said it would be a good opportunity. She talked to my teachers and they said they would release me as long as I made up the work when I came back."

Bobby and I looked at each other. Both of us wondering what to say.

"What about the investigation?" Bobby asked. "We're a team. You can't leave. You're part of us, like the three Musketeers."

"When will you be leaving?" I asked.

"I think in about a week."

I felt sad, like a part of me was taken away. What would we do without Sonny? Even if we weren't playing detective, he was like a brother who knew everything.

"It'll only be for two weeks," Sonny said. "Keep investigating. Don't give up. When I come back you can fill me in and we'll get to the bottom of everything."

Sonny left at the end of the week. We watched as he and Mrs. Griffin walked up the hill toward the subway station both of them carrying a suitcase. Sonny turned and waved goodbye. Mrs. Henderson stood nearby watching, too. She had tears in her eyes. She blew her nose. This was the first time she'd been separated from her son since he was born, she told us.

"He'll be back before you know it," she said confidently, patting Bobby and me on the back before she turned to go in.

We sat down on the stoop.

"What do we do now?" I asked.

"We'll come up with something."

Just then we spotted Mr. Moore coming down the block carrying a cage. This time I saw what was in it, a turtle, a big turtle that I knew was illegal because my teacher told us that you couldn't own a turtle as large as that in the U.S.

Bobby saw it too. We were silent as we watched him go into the building.

*****

Thanks to my little brothers, our problem was solved. Kevin and Kyle came home all excited one day.

"Sis, I bet you can't guess where we been?" said Kevin.

"Grandma's gonna be mad. You were supposed to come home right after school. Where've you been?"

"We been up at Mr. Moore's apartment. You know, the man who lives upstairs," said Kyle, grinning from ear to ear.

I sat up quickly, "As the World Turns," my favorite soap on TV forgotten.

"What do you mean you been in his apartment?" Grandma came into the room, sat down in the rocking chair and picked up her knitting needles. "Who you talking about? You know your daddy said not to go into a strange man's apartment?" She was working on sweaters to give each of us for Christmas which was months away.

Kevin and Kyle looked over at me, wanting me to get them out of trouble. "You boys better get to your homework," I said. I'd catch up with them later. They scrambled from the living room, a grateful look on their faces. After a while, I followed them into their room and closed the door.

"How did you get in? Did he open the door for you?"

"Sis. You should've seen it. He had one room filled with animals in cages and birds flying around the ceiling. It was something else," said Kevin.

"Yeah, and he even has snakes," Kyle shivered, his arms wrapped around his body like he was cold.

"Did he invite you in?" I asked. And why? I wondered. Kyle shrugged and looked over at Kevin.

"We were coming up the stairs when all of a sudden we saw an ugly cat dash out of his apartment," said Kevin jumping up and down on his bed.

"It didn't look like a cat to me. It had brown fur all over its body and beady red eyes. And it had a long body," Kyle said holding up his hands to show how big it was.

"And it was fast," Kevin said.

"What do you mean 'fast'?"

"It ran towards us and we almost didn't catch up with it."

"But you did?"

"Yeah. Kevin caught it just as it was getting away."

"So how did you get into Mr. Moore's apartment?"

"He was chasing it, too, but we caught it," said Kyle.

"And Mr. Moore invited you up to his place?"

"Kevin had to hold onto the cat or it would have got away again. He carried it inside. Mr. Moore showed him where to put it. In this room in the back of his apartment."

"Yeah, Sis. You should see it."

"What else did you see in there?" My heart was beating like I'd been running up and down the stairs.

Kyle said, "I saw some birds flying around near the ceiling."

"And I saw what looked like a baby alligator."

"A baby alligator?" I repeated.

"And a couple of snakes," said Kevin.

"You're making this up," I said

"No, we're not. That's what we saw."

"What did Mr. Moore say?"

"He made us promise not to tell anybody. He said if the neighbors find out, he'll have to leave," said Kevin.

"He's right about that," I said. What kind of man would keep animals in his small apartment, snakes, alligators, and things? I wondered.

"What are you all talking about," Grandma stood in the doorway, her hands on her hips.

"I'm just asking them about school," I said hating to lie to her. If I didn't I'd get the boys into trouble.

"What should we do?" Kevin asked after Grandma left.

Kyle looked up at me with his big brown eyes. "Don't tell Daddy, please."

I hugged him, "I won't tell anyone. Now I don't want you two going up to Mr. Moore's place again. Agreed?" We high-fived.

Wait till I tell Bobby, I thought.

Chapter Three

About a week after Sonny left, Bobby got a postcard from him. He came over to show me. On one side was this huge campus like I'd seen on TV filled with large trees and important looking buildings. On the other side, Sonny had scrawled a note.

"He says he got a tour of some music schools and Mrs. Griffin introduced him to some people she knew from when she used to live there," Bobby said.

"I didn't know she lived in Boston."

I didn't know much about Mrs. Griffith's past except what Bobby and Sonny told me. She's a nice old lady and I knew she did a lot of things when she was young and that she had important friends. Sonny said she taught them about the Harlem

Renaissance, Marcus Garvey and other things. When I met her, she was getting over a bad illness so it was a long time before she invited us into her apartment again. As soon as she got her strength back, she decided to do something special for Sonny. She told us that when they returned, she planned to help Bobby and me figure out what we wanted to do with our future.

"I hope they'll be back soon," I said. Then I remembered what Kevin and Kyle said and I told Bobby.

"That settles it. Now we've got to go introduce ourselves and find out what's going on," he said.

We put our heads together to decide when we'd go up to meet Mr. Moore.

"Let's go Saturday," said Bobby.

"I don't know if I can. I've got to go shopping with my grandma."

"You're not going to be gone all day, are you?"

"I hope not. And how do we know he'll be home?" Bobby could tell I wasn't exactly excited about this new project. And I wasn't and I didn't know why. I did want to know what was going on, but I guess my mind was on school and getting good grades especially in my English class. Finally, I agreed to go to Mr. Moore's apartment on Saturday. after I went grocery shopping with Grandma.

The weekend came too fast if you ask me. By that afternoon, Kevin, Kyle and me helped Grandma unpack the groceries and put them away. Daddy's usually off on Saturday. If he's not trying to catch up on his sleep, he's visiting his friends or spending time with Mr. Thompson, Bobby's father, at the garage working on cars.

Around three, I dashed over to Bobby's place and knocked on the door. His sister Brenda answered, phone in her hand, she's always talking to her friends on the phone.

"Bobby," she yelled over her shoulder. "Your little friend is here."

Mrs. Thompson peeked out from the kitchen. "Brenda, are you still on the phone. You've been on that telephone all morning. What if somebody else gets a call." She said hi and asked if I wanted a soda or some chips.

"How's your family?" She asked, drying her hands on a towel.

"Fine, thank you." I wondered why Bobby was taking so long to come.

"He's in the bathroom," Mrs. Thompson said. "He should be right out. Been in there a while reading comic books, no doubt. Bobby!" she called. "Maxine is here."

"Be right out." I heard him say. Then I heard the toilet flush.

"You ready?" Bobby asked leading the way to the door.

"Yeah. As ready as I can be."

"Where're you two going?" Brenda shouted.

"None of your business!" Bobby yelled back at her. And we bounced down the stairs. I felt my stomach flutter as we walked towards my building.

"You sure we should do this?" I asked.

"Yep. The Bradhurst Gumshoes are on the case," Bobby walked ahead with a confidence I didn't feel.

Just outside Mr. Moore's door, it was decided that I'd knock, tell him that I knew about my brothers visiting him and that I knew he had animals inside that we wanted to see.

"Why me?" I asked Bobby. "Why do I have to take the lead?"

"'Cause your brothers were the ones who met him first. You just want to introduce yourself, us, to make sure he knows they got family in the building."

"Don't you think he knows already. He's been here almost a month. He's seen us sitting out on the stoop. He's even seen me looking down at him from the window."

"Come on. Just knock. I'll back you up"

So I did. I knocked and knocked. No answer. I was relieved. Just as we were about to give up, I heard the latches being thrown. My stomach fluttered again and I thought I lost my voice. The door opened a crack and Mr. Moore peeked out.

"Can I help you?" he said looking down at Bobby and me.

"Good afternoon, Sir," I said clearing my voice. I know I sounded weak, like a tiny mouse. "You met my little brothers the other day and I thought I'd come up and introduce myself, welcome you to the neighborhood."

"Me, too," said Bobby.

I couldn't see his whole body, just his head and his scraggly mustache.

"That's very nice of you. Now if you'll excuse me, I'm sort of busy."

Behind him I saw a bird fly by and I heard something growling behind him.

"You got birds?" Bobby asked.

Mr. Moore cleared his throat, glanced back into his apartment nervously. "Just two lovebirds."

"Her brothers said you got alligators, snakes, and other wild animals in there," said Bobby. I knew he was getting confident.

Mr. Moore gave another nervous laugh.

"You're mistaken. That's just the TV."

"But Kevin and Kyle said they saw other animals in your apartment," I said not the least bit sure of myself.

Just then we heard someone coming up the stairs. Mr. Moore's eyes grew wide. He almost slammed the door in our face but Bobby was standing too close and would have yelled out if the door slammed on his foot. Mr. Moore did the next best thing. He threw open the door and pulled us inside.

Chapter Four

The apartment looked like ours, same layout, I mean. The front door opened onto the living room. It looked bigger than ours because he didn't have much furniture, just an old worn brown couch that looked like it had seen better days, a small TV set sitting on a table, and two chairs on each side of the window. Two doors led to the bedrooms and at the end of the hall was the kitchen and bathroom. One door was cracked open. Out of the corner of my eye, I thought I saw something move. I jumped.

Mr. Moore ran over and closed the door quickly.

"Could we see your animals?" Bobby asked.

"Animals?" Mr. Moore repeated. "I don't have any animals, just my lovebirds."

I edged towards the front door, signaling to Bobby that it was time to go.

"Sorry we troubled you, Mr. Moore," I said.

"Just one peek," said Bobby. "We won't tell anybody."

That's when we heard some growling and it sounded like two animals fighting. Mr. Moore quickly dashed into the other room. Bobby followed close behind. I did too. What I saw, I couldn't believe my eyes.

There were cages stacked on top of cages. A few were empty. Inside two of them were animals I didn't recognize. In one big fish tank I saw two small snakes, in another a large lizard. I felt goose bumps on my arms. They gave me the creeps.

"Let's go." I pulled Bobby's arm.

He moved away following Mr. Moore to the other side of the room where the neighbor was carrying a small monkey, trying to put him back into a cage.

Bobby grabbed another animal and held it while Mr. Moore opened the door to another cage and put it in.

Once everything had settled down, he explained that the two animals that had gotten out of their cages were a spider monkey and a ferret.

"I've got to get better locks." Glancing around at the other cages, he smiled nervously,

Bobby stood in front of a fish tank, his nose practically pressing against the glass. "Is that a python?"

"No, it's a baby boa constrictor," Mr. Moore explained.

I was standing next to another tank when out of the corner of my eye, I saw something move. It was an ugly looking spider, black with fuzzy legs and it seemed to be staring at me. I jumped, bumping into Bobby.

"It's a Chilean rose haired tarantula. It won't hurt you." Mr. Moore moved around the room answering Bobby's questions, telling him about each animal.

"This is a monitor lizard, and in this tank is a baby alligator." He was smiling proudly showing off his pets. I hadn't moved from the door. Bobby was in a trance, like he was in Disneyland.

"I want to go home," I finally said loudly so that they could hear me. They both turned and stared at me as if this was the first time they'd ever saw me.

"I'm sorry," Mr. Moore said. "Of course." He opened the door and led us back out into the living room. "Please don't tell anyone about what you've seen. I don't want to have to move again."

"We won't, promise," Bobby said turning to me and nodding his head. "Do you mind if we come back again?"

"If you promise you'll keep my secret." He rubbed Bobby's head and shook both of our hands.

When we were downstairs in my apartment, I said, "I'm not going back up there. I'm scared of all those animals."

"There's nothing to be afraid of. They're in cages. They can't hurt you."

"I don't care. You can go back if you want. But not me."

He called me a scaredy-cat. "I can't wait until Sonny gets back," he said as he left.

Chapter Five

A week passed and Sonny hadn't come back. Bobby went up to Mr. Moore's every day. When he first stopped by to ask if I wanted to go upstairs, I told him I didn't. He didn't ask me anymore.

We walked home together from school and after putting down his books and changing his clothes, he'd race up to Mr. Moore's apartment. I asked him about it and he said the neighbor taught him about the animals, what they ate and how they acted.

"The spider monkey is a lot of fun. And the ferret, they're always getting out of their cages and getting into fights. Mr. Moore and me would chase them around the apartment while the lovebird flew around the ceiling pooping on everything. It's crazy."

"What about the tarantula? Is it poisonous?"

"It hasn't bitten me though it feels funny as it crawls on my finger. You should come up. There's nothing to be scared about."

"No thanks. I don't mind dogs or gold fish. But those strange animals..."

"Mr. Moore calls them exotic. He gets them from the pet store downtown. He said the owner lets him buy them at a discount. He lets me feed them. I think he would like to share his pets with other people. But he told me he had to leave his last place when the neighbors complained. When they found out about his pets, they screamed bloody murder. Said they weren't paying rent to live in a zoo, and that his animals were dangerous, dirty, noisy and smelled up the place."

I could understand, but I didn't tell Bobby.

"Those pets are his family. He loves them."

"Doesn't he have any relatives?"

"I don't know. I think he has a sister who lives over in New Jersey."

We stopped in front of my building.

"Have you heard from Sonny?" I asked.

"I heard my mom talking to Mrs. Henderson and she said Mrs. Griffin asked permission to enroll him into an academy for two weeks down south somewhere, so I guess he won't be back for a while."

"Max, are you down there? I thought I heard your voice."

I looked up and saw Grandma, her head sticking out the third-floor window.

"Yes, Grandma," I said.

"I need you to run and get something from the store for me."

"I gotta go," I told Bobby and dashed upstairs.

"I'll be up at Mr. Moore's if you change your mind. It's educational."

"I'll pass."

Chapter Six

On my way to the store, I spotted Mr. Moore. He was carrying a big box. "Afternoon, Miss Johnson." As he passed, he winked at me.

I smiled. Watching him go up the steps and into the building, I wondered if it was another animal.

"Smells like a pigsty," I heard our neighbor, Mr. Carter grumble as he passed me on his way out. I shifted the groceries to my other arm so I could squeeze through the door before it closed. I took in a breath. I hadn't noticed before but it did smell different, not like the smells coming from the trashcans on trash day, the sour smell of rotting garbage. It reminded me of when I was little and went to visit my grandparents on my mother's side. They lived in Virginia on a farm way out in the woods. They raised horses, goats, and pigs. The hallway smelled sorta like that. If Mr. Moore didn't want the neighbors to discover his pets, he'd have to do something about that.

Before climbing up to our apartment, I stood still, listening to see if I could hear sounds from Mr. Moore's apartment. I heard the sound of a truck going by on the street and Carole and her friends jumping Double-Dutch a few doors down. Their voices were loud. I could hear muffled voices coming from the neighbors' apartments and when I strained to listen, I could hear birds chirping and a low growl. I decided to tell Bobby. Maybe he could mention it to Mr. Moore.

"You got everything on the list?" Grandma asked taking the groceries out the bag as I put them away.

"I couldn't find the sausages you like but I got everything else."

"Guess I'll have to make something else," she said.

After making myself a peanut butter and jelly sandwich, I sat down at the kitchen table to do my homework. Just as I was getting started, Bobby knocked his familiar knock on the door. Kevin ran to open it.

"Can't stay long," Bobby said, plopping down on the chair opposite me. "My mom's been bugging me about my grade in my science class. The teacher called and told her I wasn't turning in homework. I got a science project due in a week and since Sonny isn't around, I thought maybe you could give me some ideas."

I shrugged. "I'm not good at science. I could help you with English though."

"I don't need no help with English. I'm doing okay in that class. It's science that I need help with."

If Sonny were here, he'd come up with all sorts of ideas, I was sure, but he's not. Changing the subject, I mentioned the neighbor's complaint about the smell in the hallway.

"I never noticed," Bobby said absently. His chin in his hands, he stared down at the table. "Maybe I could do something about space. Maybe I could build a model of the planets revolving around the sun. Naw, that would take too much time and I don't have material. Or I could do that experiment where you take baking soda and do something with it."

"Why don't you interview Mr. Moore about his pets and do a report on one of them like the ferret or the baby alligator. You could draw pictures and show what they eat and other things."

"Yeah, I could do that!" His face brightened. "Can you come upstairs with me while I ask him. You could help me think up questions and if you have a camera, take some pictures."

"I'm sorta busy studying for a math test tomorrow."

"It won't take long, please."

I couldn't let him down, so I put my books away and followed him up to Mr. Moore's apartment. I heard Grandma telling me to hurry back to help with dinner.

Mr. Moore was happy to see us.

"Come in, young folks. I'd like to show you the newest editions to the family."

I hung back as they went into the pets' room. "Com'on," Bobby said, "we won't be long." I didn't want to, but I followed.

Mr. Moore reached his hand into a new fish tank, a little smaller than the other two tanks where the monitor lizard and the boa constrictor stared at me. He picked up one of the tiny snakes and it curled around his hand. It was no bigger than his palm. He stroked it gently. I shivered. Then he handed it over to Bobby who let it curl around his finger. He lifted the thing up to his face and stared into its eyes.

"Would you like to hold the other one?" Mr. Moore asked me.

"No, thank you," I said, my voice sounded weak as I moved towards the door.

"Mr. Moore, Bobby has to do a science project and he was wondering if you'd let him do it on one of your pets," I said, glaring at Bobby who paid me no attention. He kept stroking the snake.

"Why sure. No problem," Mr. Moore said as he took the snake from Bobby, put it back into the tank and headed for the outer door.

Once in the living room, he offered us some soda and cookies. I shook my head, Bobby nodded yes. While Mr. Moore was in the kitchen, I gestured to Bobby that he should wash his hands. He just shrugged and grabbed a cookie from the plate Mr. Moore had placed on the table.

"Now, which animal would you like to do a report on," Mr. Moore asked, getting comfortable in the wing chair opposite us.

"Oh, I don't know," Bobby said, wiping crumbs off his shirt.

"What about the spider monkey or the Chilean rose-haired tarantula? Either of them would make a good subject. You could do a report on the baby alligator or even the monitor lizard. Or even the boa constrictor." He uncrossed his legs and reached for a cookie.

"Mr. Moore," I asked leaning forward. "How did you get interested in exotic pets?"

He shifted in his chair. "Well, I've always been interested in animals since I was a child. I grew up on a farm in Alabama. We had pigs, goats, chickens, the usual domestic animals you see on a farm. When I came up to the city, since I didn't know anybody, I use to watch a lot of TV. Nature shows attracted me, and still do, shows like "Wild

Kingdom" with Marlin Perkins, and "Zoo Parade" that feature wild and exotic animals. One of the first documentaries I watched was a science program called, "The Nature of Things."

"I like animal shows, too," Bobby said.

"Every day I passed this pet store downtown not far from where I work. I'd stop and look into the store window. One day I decided to go in and look around. I did this for about a month until the owner comes up to me and asks if I'd like to buy one of the animals. I didn't know what to say. I couldn't afford any and I didn't know anything about them, how to care for them or anything."

"What did you do?" I asked.

"Did you save up and buy one?" Bobby asked.

"No, at first I went to the library and started looking up information about lovebirds, they were my first. Then I went back to the store and purchased those two you see flying around in the room. I don't keep them in a cage so you can see the mess they make. I try to confine them to the back room," he smiled. "Sometimes, they get out when I forget to close the door."

"Did they cost you a lot?" Bobby asked. "I'd like to have a couple of birds but I don't think my parents would let me."

"Tell us about the other animals you collected," I asked

"Next came the monitor lizard, and then the baby alligator. They are fairly easy to take care of because I keep them in fish tanks. The spider monkey and the ferret cause me the most trouble but their good company. They keep getting out of their cages, as you know."

"What do you feed them," I asked.

"The snakes and lizard, I feed them feeder mice. I buy some dog food for the ferret and I give him scrapes from the table like liver, kidney and bones. I give the spider monkey fruit, seeds and honey. Providing for my pets can cost a lot of my paycheck. But the store owner gives me a discount since I'm a regular customer and we've gotten to know each other over the years."

He turned to Bobby, "Have you decided on what animal you want to do a report on?" Bobby, who was stuffing his mouth with cookies, stopped chewing.

"I think I'd like to do a report on the bald python," he grinned.

"Well, I guess you'd better get started researching them. I'll help you as much as I can," Mr. Moore stood up.

"Thank you for helping us," I said getting up too and moving towards the front door. Bobby was looking at the door to the pet room. "Com'on," I said, grabbing his arm. "I gotta go finish studying for my test tomorrow."

"Can I come up and ask you more questions, Mr. Moore?"

"Sure you can and you can help me feed my pets, too." he said opening the door. He shook my hand and patted Bobby on the back.

"Why didn't you tell him about the smells?" I asked as we walked down to my apartment.

"You should have held the bald python. I think I'm in love."

"You're so crazy."

Chapter Seven

I was walking home from school when Bobby caught up with me just as I was turning the corner to our block.

"Didn't you hear me calling you?" he said, jumping in front of me and breathing hard. I kept walking. He walked backwards almost bumping into a trashcan.

"Nope," I said. "I was thinking about the English paper I need to write. It's due on Monday."

"Mr. Moore has to visit his sister in Jersey. It's an emergency." He matched my steps.

"So?" I asked, glancing over at him. It didn't mean anything to me. "What does Mr. Moore going to Jersey have to do with you?"

"He asked me to look after his pets while he's gone. You know, make sure they get food and water."

"Good for you," I said. We were coming up to his apartment building. "How long will he be gone?"

"Just a few days. He's leaving early tomorrow morning. He'll be back on Friday. I'm going up to his apartment and he's gonna give me last minute instructions. Wanna come?"

"No thank you. You know I don't like those strange animals."

"Aw, com'on. They're not strange."

"I gotta get started on my paper." I stepped towards my building.

"It won't take long and I really need your help. Please."

His hands folded together like he was praying; he stuck his face close to mine. His breath smelled like peppermint gum.

 "Pretty please. You're good at remembering things, and besides, Mr. Moore will feel better if he knows they'll be two of us."

"Well," I felt myself giving in. I laughed when he crossed his eyes and made a silly face. "I'll come but I won't touch those animals."

He kissed me on the cheek and took off running into his building. "I'll knock on your door later tonight. You won't have to do nothing, just listen and make sure I don't forget what he tells me."

How am I gonna explain to Grandma why I gotta go out tonight? I heard her and Daddy talking about Mr. Moore the other morning when he came in from work. After she gave him an update about how we were doing, she told him Kevin and Kyle were talking about seeing our neighbor carrying boxes upstairs. "Something's strange about that man," Grandma said.

Daddy sat at the kitchen table as Grandma fixed him breakfast. She always makes him a hearty meal when he comes in from having worked all night. He looked so tired, could barely keep his eyes open as he dug into his plate.

"Mornin' Daddy, Grandma," I said as I slid in the chair opposite him.

"Mornin' Sweetheart." He leaned over and gave me a peck on the cheek.

"How's school?" he asked. Before I could answer, Grandma interrupted.

"Did you wake Kevin and Kyle up and tell them they better be getting ready for school?" She turned away from me and shouted towards the hallway. "Kevin, Kyle. You boys better be up and in the bathroom washing up."

I told Daddy about how I was keeping my grades up.

"That's my girl." He patted me on the back as he finished off his plate. Getting up, he carried his plate over to the sink. Grandma slid a couple of pancakes in front of me, and sat down to drink her coffee. First Kevin, then Kyle half-dressed dragged themselves into the kitchen. Still in their pajamas, they didn't look like they'd washed anything, combed their hair or even brushed their teeth. I could see the crust from last night's sleep in the corners of their eyes.

"Boys, you heard your grandmother. Get back in there, finish washing up."

"Aw Daddy, we washed up," Kevin said.

"And we brushed our teeth," Kyle whined.

"Don't get no breakfast 'till you do," Grandma said.

I finished eating, put my plate in the sink. "Com'on boys, I'm gonna make sure you clean behind your ears.

"We can do it ourselves." They started to race into the bathroom to see who could get there first.

"Wait, boys." Daddy stopped them. He squatted down between them. "You boys minding your Grandma and sister? Not giving them a hard time?"

"Yes, Daddy," They said together. He hugged them and let them go.

"I'm off to bed," he said kissing Grandma and me on the cheek.

"That man works too hard," Grandma said as we watched him stagger to his bedroom. He'd sleep most of the day until just a few hours before he had to go back to work. When I get older, I'm gonna get a job and take care of all my family so my daddy won't have to work so hard.

I went to the sink and started washing the dishes.

"Leave 'em. You go get ready for school."

Kevin and Kyle came racing back to the table.

"Shhhh," I said, "Daddy's gone to bed. You know we got to be quiet."

Grandma placed a plate of pancakes before them. I poured them glasses of milk and orange juice. "Bow your heads and say grace," I told them just as they were about to tackle their breakfast.

Then I went in and finished getting ready for school. This was our morning routine.

Now tonight I got to go with Bobby up to Mr. Moore's so he can get last minute instructions on taking care of the neighbor's precious pets. I wasn't looking forward to that.

*****

Like Bobby said, it didn't take long for Mr. Moore to show Bobby and me what to do, though I was barely listening, keeping my eyes on the clock, holding my nose, and watching to see that those lovebirds didn't poop on my head. Except for them, all the other animals were in their cages.

"Any questions?" Mr. Moore asked looking down at us. Bobby shook his head eagerly.

"I'll take good care of them till you get back."

"I won't be gone long, just till Saturday morning if all goes well. My sister Mabel fell down and broke her hip. She had to be rushed to the hospital. I gotta look after her plants and animals," he smiled. "She loves cats, dogs and plants. Got an apartment so full you can hardly walk around. So I'm not surprised to hear she had an accident. She's up in age, you know. After our parents died, she practically raised me, my brother and my younger sister Bernice."

"I didn't know you had family," I said.

"Everybody's got family," Bobby looked at me like I'd lost my mind.

"I don't mean that. I mean..."

"I know what you mean," Mr. Moore said. "It's because I care so much about my pets you wouldn't think I had anybody else. They are my family, too."

I wondered why they couldn't take care of Miss Mabel's animals and plants but before I could think to ask, he broke in.

"My sister Bernice lives out in California. I don't know where my brother Thomas lives. Haven't seen either one of them in years. Mabel and me, while we don't see each other much, at least we keep in touch and if either of us needs anything we're just a phone call away." He stood up. "I'd better let you children go. It's getting late and I have to pack."

I glanced over at Bobby who was nodding off. I punched him in his side. He jumped up.

"We'll keep everything in order. Nothing to worry about," he said as he stretched and covered his mouth to try to keep from yawning.

"One more thing, I almost forgot." Mr. Moore disappeared into the other bedroom.

"Do you remember what to do?" I whispered to Bobby once Mr. Moore had gone.

"Not everything. But with you helping me..."

"Here's a spare key. Just remember to look in on them twice a day to make sure everything's okay. Oh, and here's the number where you can reach me in case of an emergency." Mr. Moore handed Bobby the key and a slip of paper.

"You don't know how much I appreciate this. I hate to leave my pets all alone for any length of time but I'm sure they'll be all right. " He walked us to the door.

"You don't have nothing to worry about. Me and Max will look after them like they're our own." Bobby shook his hand.

"I hope your sister will get better soon," I said.

Once we had reached my apartment, I asked Bobby, "Are you sure you can handle all this?"

"No problem. Like I said, we're the Bradhurst Gumshoes. No challenge is too hard for us." He grinned as he dashed down to the street. I wished Sonny were here. Three heads are better than two especially when one is like Bobby who doesn't think before he rushes into a burning building. I shook my head.

Chapter Eight

Early the next morning, I glanced out the window and saw Mr. Moore leave, carrying a suitcase and heading up the hill to the subway. I had just finished eating breakfast when Bobby pounded on the door with his usual knock.

"Mornin' Bobby," Grandma said. "You're up early. Had your breakfast yet?"

Bobby shook his head though he eyed my pancakes and I could see his mouth watering. "No thanks. I already ate." He turned to me, "You ready?"

"For what? I gotta finish getting ready for school." I got up from the table, placed my dish into the sink and picked up my book bag.

"I know. But before we go, we gotta check on Mr. Moore's pets," Bobby whispered.

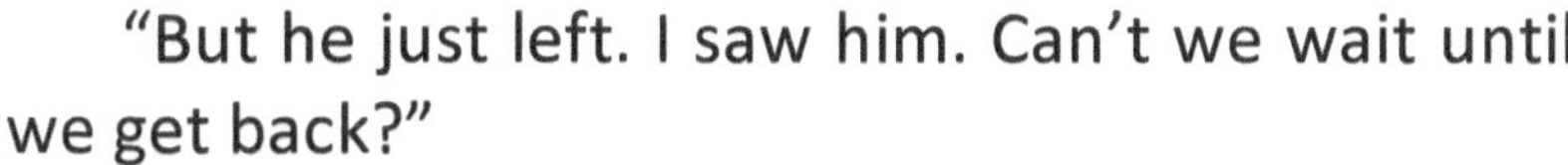

"But he just left. I saw him. Can't we wait until we get back?"

Bobby's shoulders slumped. "I guess you're right." He turned to go. I kissed Grandma on the cheek. Kevin and Kyle had already left.

"Wait up," I called to Bobby, catching up with him as he reached the outside door.

I had to run to keep up with him. He does everything fast- walk, eat, talk. We reached school just in time to hear the first bell ring. We agreed we'd meet right after school and go up to Mr. Moore's apartment to take care of his pets.

*****

After dropping my books down, I walked upstairs to the neighbor's apartment. Bobby was waiting outside the door for me. He reached into his pocket and searched for Mr. Moore's key.

"I know it's in here somewhere," he said as he dug in all his jean pockets pulling out chewing gum wrappers, dirty tissues, a skate key, his apartment key, a toy whistle, the stub of a pencil, a toy car.

"You sure you got it? You didn't leave it at home?"

With everything spread out on the steps, he knelt down and rummaged through the pile. Finally, he found it, stuck in the toy car.

"Told you," he said, as he put the key into the lock and turned.

"Don't forget your stuff," I said as he opened the door.

He looked down at the steps, "Oh yeah, thanks." He gathered everything up and crammed them into his pocket.

Mr. Moore's apartment was just as it was last evening except it was quiet. All the doors were closed. If you didn't know, you wouldn't think he had a room filled with animals, though it still smelled like a zoo. I tried not to breathe in too deeply.

"Com'on" Bobby said, leading the way to the pet room. I hung back, not ready for what we would find when he opened the door.

No sooner did he push open the door when the noise started. The lovebirds who were locked in their cage, fluttered their wings furiously up against the bars, the monkey leaped around in his cage, shaking the bars like he was about to bust out of jail, the ferret walked up and down in his cage, back and forth like my history teacher did when she was thinking. Only the monitor lizard seemed to be asleep in his tank. He didn't even glance out way. I didn't see the tarantula. She must have been hiding under the pile of straw in the corner of her tank. Bobby put water in all the cages just as Mr. Moore had told him. He didn't release the lovebirds nor the monkey or the ferret. But when he came to the two bald pythons, he reached into the tank and picked one up.

"Isn't she beautiful?" he said as he watched the snake curl around his hand and slither through his fingers.

"Yuk" I jumped back. "Please put it back."

He pushed it towards me. "Com'on. She's harmless. Touch her."

"How can you tell it's a she?" I asked edging further away.

"Mr. Moore said her name is Carmela."

"What about the other one. Is that a male or female and what's its name?" I couldn't believe I was even asking that.

He put Carmela back in the tank and picked up the other one.

"It's a she and her name is Melo." He stroked its back.

"How can you tell the difference? They look the same to me." I couldn't take my eyes off them.

"That's because you aren't looking at them closely. Look at the color and the markings." He held it up to my face. I pulled back.

"Can we go now. It's getting late."

He put Melo back in the tank and picked up Carmela and dropped her into his jacket pocket.

"What are you doing! You're not taking it with you."

He looked around the room at the cages and tanks making sure everything was in order, switched off the light and stepped into the living room. I followed close behind him. Glad to be away from the animals.

"Bobby, you forgot the snake in your pocket."

"No, I didn't. I'm taking it to school tomorrow for a show and tell."

"You can't do that. What if Mr. Moore finds out?"

"He won't be back for a few days. I'm just gonna take her to show to my science class. There's no harm in that. Right?"

"I don't know about that," I said as I followed Bobby down to the first floor. "I don't think it's a good idea."

He waved me off as he hopped down the steps and taking the bald python out of his pocket, he yelled back at me. "Everybody is gonna be blown out of their minds."

I shook my head as I turned and went back inside. I couldn't believe what he was planning to do. I shivered thinking about the bald python in his pocket. Glad I wasn't in his science class.

Chapter Nine

I didn't see Bobby at school the next day. He's not in any of my classes. But sometimes I'd see him lunchtime or playing basketball with his friend from over on 8th Ave. I didn't know them though I'd see them at the park playing ball or skating. On the way back from school I was wondering if he made it there especially since he said he had a science project due. And even more especially since he had taken Mr. Moore's snake to school. As I was nearing his building I saw him sitting on the stoop, his head in his hands.

"You got home early?" I asked sitting down beside him. I could tell by the look on his face that something was wrong. He looked as if he'd lost his best friend.

"Are you sick? Is everybody in your family all right?"

I thought about Sonny. Has anything happened to him? Bobby never looks depressed unless his parents had grounded him. He always has an excited look on his face ready for the next adventure.

"What's wrong?" I asked again.

"You were right. I shouldn't have took Carmela to school?"

"Why? What happened? Didn't your teacher like it?"

"Everybody was excited, wanting to hold her. I passed her around the class then I put her back in my pocket or I thought I did."

"What do you mean?"

He didn't look at me. When he finally did, I saw tears in his eyes.

"Did Carmela die? Is she hurt? Where is she? Did you lose her?"

He sighed and put his hands over his face.

"Yeah, when I got home, I couldn't find her. I thought she was in my pocket but she wasn't. I looked everywhere. What am I gonna tell Mr. Moore when he comes back day after tomorrow?"

I almost wanted to say I told you so, but I didn't. Instead I told him like my grandma always tells us to try to retrace our steps.

"Go back to where you last saw the little snake."

"Last time I had her was in my science class, I think."

"You sure you got it back? Maybe somebody in your class took her."

He thought for a moment. "I don't think so. I remember Mrs. Clifford, my science teacher, told me to put her away. Then Jacko did his show and tell. I felt her in my pocket when I went to my English class."

"Did you take her out to show to anybody?"

"I can't remember."

"Do you think you lost her on your way home from school?"

He said he didn't think so. "You gotta help me find her before Mr. Moore gets back."

As it was still early, we started walking back to P.S. 194 looking everywhere along the way. Where would a little snake be? I didn't have much hope in finding her. We looked under garbage cans and in alleyways. Even as we crossed 8th Avenue we looked to see if anything lay smashed in the gutters. By the time we got to school, everyone had gone home and the school yard was empty.

We tried the front door but it was locked.

"Let's go around to the back," Bobby said dashing away from me. I followed. Keeping up with him wasn't easy because he was practically running.

"What about the fence. It's usually locked," I said out of breath. The fence was over 7 feet. An old sturdy lock connected the chain together. Bobby kicked at it, shook it, then not giving up, he started to climb.

"I know you don't expect me to follow you?" I looked up at him. He was half way to the top. I had on my good skirt and I wasn't about to climb a fence.

"You scared? Come on. I need your help." He jumped down on the other side and stood there looking at me, his hands on his hips. Then he ran along the fence until he found a spot where the fence was coming apart. He was able to pull it up from the bottom and told me to squeeze through.

"What about my bookbag? I can't just leave it here. Somebody might take it."

"Don't worry about that. We gotta get inside and look for Carmela."

I followed him into the basement door which was propped open. And stashed my bag behind the stairs.

He raced ahead, up to the second floor taking two steps at a time. I was out of breath by the time I caught up with him. He signaled for me to stop.

Mr. Jones, the custodian, was just going into one classroom propping the door open with a big trash can. He set a small radio on the ledge and was humming softly, a cigarette dangling out the side of his mouth. When he disappeared into the classroom, Bobby and me snuck past.

Luckily, he had unlocked all the doors on the floor to make it easier to move from one room to the other. The Science Lab was at the far end of the hallway. It would probably take Mr. Jones at least 15 minutes to get to it.

"I thought you said you lost it in your English class."

"I'm not sure. You start at the back of the room and I'll start at the front," he said. "We got to look in all the desk in case Carmela is in one of them. "

The thought of finding the bald Python didn't sound appealing to me. She could stay lost as far as I was concerned, but I knew if we didn't get the snake back to Mr. Moore, Bobby would be in trouble.

We search the whole room but no Carmela.

"Let's try my English class."

We started down the hall listening for Mr. Jones. He was coming closer. I could tell by the sound of the trash can wheels rumbling along and music from his radio that grew louder the closer he came.

"It's just around this corner."

As we passed Mrs. Ellis room, my English class, I stopped and peered in. Bobby grabbed me by the arm and pulled me along. We came to room 201 where Bobby's class was.

Most of the classrooms looked the same. Rows of desks in the middle and along the sides book cases filled with books, and in the front of the room, the teacher's desk next to the chalkboard. Miss

Baxter had added her own decorations on the walls, a poster of the Egyptian pyramids, one of the Eifel Tower in Paris, and another of the Milky Way. I liked this room. It looked comfortable compared to Mrs. Ellis's room. Her room was filled with plants and composition papers we'd written pinned to the walls. His teacher had sayings plastered above the board,

"Max, we don't have time for you to sightsee. Start looking over by the bookcase. I'll check the desks," Bobby said, his voice anxious. "We gotta find her."

I flipped through the books on one shelf. "If she's in one of these, she's gonna be one smart snake." I laughed.

I heard Mr. Jones rumbling trash can and he was singing along with the song on the radio.

"He's coming this way," Bobby whispered. "We gotta hide." We scrambled over to the closet and closed the door just as the custodian walked in. The closet was filled with boxes and I don't know what else. I could see Mr. Jones through the cracks in the door. He emptied the wastebaskets and the pencil sharpener. Then he started wiping down each desk. Suddenly I felt something crawl up my leg. I started to scream. Bobby put his hand over my mouth.

"Carmela," he whispered, gently taking the snake from my leg. It's a wonder Mr. Jones didn't hear us. He stopped and look around. Then he continued what he was doing and when he finished, he turned out the lights, closed the door locking it behind him.

Bobby stroked the snake, kissed it and put it in his pocket.

"Let's get out of here," Bobby said hurrying to the door.

"Wait! we gotta make sure he's gone."

"You're right." He slowly opened the door and peered into the hallway. The custodian was in the classroom a few doors away. "Let's go."

We raced in the opposite direction, down the stairs where I picked up my bookbag and headed over to the part of the fence I'd squeezed through earlier.

When we got to our block, we sat down on my stoop.

A big smile on his face, Bobby said, "Whew! That was a close call."

"I hope you learned your lesson."

He took Carmela out of his pocket and stroked her again.

"Isn't she cute."

"See you tomorrow," I said getting up and heading to my apartment.

"Aren't you gonna come with me to put Carmela back in her cage?"

I sucked my lips. "It's late and my Grandma's gonna wonder why I'm not home from school."

"It'll only take a minute. Besides you can help me look after Mr. Moore's pets."

I dropped my bookbag at my apartment. Then I followed him up to Mr. Moore's place.

Chapter Ten

As Bobby put the key into the door, it suddenly opened.

"Well, well. This is good timing," Mr. Moore said, opening the door wider and inviting Bobby and me in.

Both of us were shocked, our mouths open. Bobby still had the key in his hand. "I thought you was coming back tomorrow," he managed to say."

"I had planned to stay but then my sister was driving me crazy. She told me to go home. She was doing much better."

He turned away, taking off his coat and throwing it over the chair. I noticed his suitcase nearby so I figured he'd just got in.

"I hope my little ones didn't give you any trouble," he said, smiling from ear to ear. He started towards the room where he kept his pets. Bobby glanced over at me, a look of panic on his face.

"Mr. Moore, can I have a glass of water," I coughed like I was choking.

"Sure, I'll just be a second. Sit down and make yourself comfortable. As soon as he went into the kitchen, I nudged Bobby. He realized what I was doing and dashed over to the room while I kept a look out. He came back in a flash just as Mr. Moore returned with a glass of water. He handed it to me. and looked over at Bobby,

"You okay, Bobby?" he asked, sitting down on the sofa. Bobby wiped the sweat on his brow and grinned.

Scratching his head, he answered, "Yeah, I'm fine now."

"Well, shall we take a look at your charge," Mr. Moore got up and headed for the room. Bobby was right on his heels. I walked behind. When he opened the door, the smell almost knocked me over.

"Let me open the window, it's a bit stuffy. Did you make sure to give them water?" Mr. Moore asked.

"Yes, I came up, gave them the food you showed me and water. Max helped," he smiled.

I saw Carmel curled up in a ball at the. corner of the tank. We watched as Mr. Moore went to each cage and examined each animal. He opened the cage and let the birds loose to fly around the room. I ducked as they flew over my head.

"I gotta get home," I told Bobby loud enough for Mr. Moore to hear. He seemed to be in another world. Bobby too ignored me. I nudged him in his ribs.

"Ow!" he scowled at me.

"I'm sorry to keep you two. I know you've got a lot of things to do." Mr. Moore reached into his pocket and pulled out his wallet. He handed us $5.00 each. "I know it's not much but you don't know how much you looking after my animals meant to me." He walked us to the door. "You're welcome to come up any time." He shook Bobby's hand and patted me on the back.

I was halfway down the stairs when he closed the door.

"We coulda stayed longer," Bobby said as I stopped by my apartment door.

"You coulda." Just as I was about to turn the key in the lock, the door opened."

"Max, where have you been? You know you supposed to come home right after school. I see your books here but not you," My grandmother grabbed my arm and started to pull me inside.

"I'm sorry. Bobby and me..." I turned to include Bobby but he was running out the downstairs door.

"Don't just stand there. Come on in, clean yourself up and help me get dinner." Grandma said.

Chapter Eleven

"What you doing this weekend?" Lillian asked as we reached the corner of my block.

"Nothing much," I said.

"My family's taking us to visit my uncle's. He's got this big house on Staten Island. We gotta take the ferry across. Have you ever been on Staten Island?" she asked.

"Not that I remember," I said. Lillian is always bragging about her family and the trips they take. Except for going down to Virginia to get my grandmother, I never been farther than the city, though Daddy promised us that one day he'd take us down to Florida to Disney World.

"Well, I gotta go before my mother comes looking for me. See you Monday and thanks for letting me borrow your homework," Lillian said as we reached the corner of my block.

She lived on the 138th Street, not far from my neighborhood, the block filled with nice looking row houses where I heard that wealthy people, professionals like doctors and lawyers lived. I watched her hurry away.

I was surprised to see Bobby sitting on his stoop looking all sad and rejected. It had been over a week since last I saw him. I was busy with after school math tutoring trying to bring up my grades.

"Hey, what's up. You didn't lose one of Mr. Moore's animals again?"

He gave me a look. "No," and shook his head.

'Then what's the matter. Have you heard from Sonny and Mrs. Griffin?

"Not yet. I think my Mom said they'd be back next week."

"Tell me, what's got you looking like you lost your best friend?" I sat down beside him.

"Mr. Moore is moving out."

I had to catch my breath. "Huh? moving, where?"

His head lowered, he looked down at his hands. "He's moving out of the city."

"Did somebody tell on him. About the animals, I mean. Did one of the neighbors rat on him?" I just couldn't believe it. He hadn't been living here that long. "Did he tell you?"

"Yeah, he said his sister fell down again and broke her hip. He said she needs someone to stay with her because she can't stay alone."

"But what about the animals? He can't just up and leave them here."

Bobby got up and started throwing a baseball in the air and catching it with his glove. "He's taking them with him. He said he and his sister were looking for a larger apartment in New Jersey and I guess she said he could probably bring his pets with him."

I sure was going to miss him even if I didn't care much for the animals. He was a nice man. And sure enough, a few days later we saw a moving truck parked in front of the apartment. Two men carried Mr. Moore's furniture and put them in the truck. I didn't see any of his pets. I guess Mr. Moore was saving them for last.

Bobby and me went upstairs to his apartment later that afternoon after the truck was gone. Bobby knocked on his door. Mr. Moore greeted us with a bright smile.

"Come in my young friends. His arm outstretched like he was an usher or something. "Sorry I can't offer you a chair. Most of my furniture has been moved to our new place in New Jersey. Everything except a chair, that small table and my bed. I'll be leaving at the end of the week." He didn't seem sad.

Bobby and me squatted, cross-legged on the floor. His eyes were on the room where Mr. Moore kept his pets. Mr. Moore sat down on the only chair.

"Thank you for coming. I'd offer you something to drink but I'm afraid my glasses are all packed up."

"What are you gonna do about your pets," I asked even though Bobby had already told me.

"Would you like to have them," he asked with a grin. "Maybe the love birds or the ferret. Or maybe the tarantula, you'd love him."

I tried to smile back at him but I felt a lump in my throat, no way.

"She don't like your pets," Bobby said. "She's scared of them."

"Besides, we're not allowed to have pets in the building," I blurted out without thinking.

"I'm just playing with you," Mr. Moore said. "I'm taking them with me to my sister's. If we're not allowed to keep them, I'll have to give them away."

"I'd take them if I could," Bobby said. "Can I say goodbye?"

"Sure can." Mr. Moore walked us over to the pet room. The animals must sense something changing because they were really upset. Though I'd gotten use to the smells and the noisy birds, seeing all those exotic animals in one room still gave me the creeps. The boa constrictor and the monitor lizard in their tanks; the monitor lizard seemed to be giving me the evil eye. Out of the corner of my eye I felt something crawl on my shoulder. I jumped ready to scream.

"Come here, Marvin. Naughty boy. How did you get out?" Mr. Moore reached over and picked up the tarantula, let it crawl along his hand, and gently placed him back into the tank. I looked around for Bobby who was real quiet, his eyes watching the ball pythons wrapped around each other in another tank

"I gotta get home," I whispered. He paid me no mind. I said it a little louder in Bobby's ear. He scowled at me.

"I forgot this is a school night. I shouldn't have kept you so long," Mr. Moore said, moving towards the door. "I'm gonna miss my two friends. Maybe one day I'll come back for a visit."

We thanked him and started down the stairs. I could have sworn I heard Bobby sniff. I didn't think those animals meant that much to him. "Sure wish Sonny was back," I said. He didn't say anything when I got to my door. "See you tomorrow," I yelled as he kept walking.

I opened my door just in time to hear grandma yell, "Maxine, is that you?"

Epilogue

Mr. Moore left on Friday. I didn't see him go with all his animals. On Saturday I went over to Bobby's to ask if he'd like to go up to Mr. Moore's apartment. His mother said he wasn't home. "He's probably over at the park," Mrs. Thompson said. I decided I'd go up to Mr. Moore's apartment by myself. Don't know what I expected to find but I was curious. The door was unlocked and as I walked in, the strong odor of the animals hit me. I sneezed and held my nose as I looked around the empty room. I heard a noise coming from the room where he kept his pets. Did he leave them behind? I wondered. Cautiously, I tip toed to the room and turned the doorknob.

Sitting in the middle of the empty room was Bobby. In his hand was Carmela, the bald python

"I was looking all over for you. What are you doing up here?" I asked.

A smile spread across Bobby's face as the tiny snake crawled between his fingers. He shrugged. "Mr. Moore left her for me."

I looked around. "You mean he just left the snake here in the room?"

Bobby explained, "Mr. Moore came up to my apartment and said he had a present for me. He asked my father if I could have it and Daddy said yes. Nobody knew what was in the box until Mr. Moore left. When I opened it up and my mother saw it, she screamed, so did Brenda. She's scared to death of snakes. My dad laughed. He wasn't scared." Bobby stroked Carmela as it curled around his fingers.

Bobby said the family had a discussion. His mother said definitely not. Finally, they came to an agreement. As long as Bobby kept the snake in the box, in his room, and he took care of it using his allowance money to buy food for it, he could keep her. but if it got out, Carmela would have to go.

"What are you two doing in here?" Mr. Brown's voice made us jump. "You're not supposed to be in here." He carried a bucket filled with different bottles, a mop and a broom. "I've got to clean this place up for the new tenants. Now git." He set his things down and threw open the windows as he moved from room to room.

'Whew, it stinks in here. Smells like a zoo."

As me and Bobby headed downstairs, Mr. Brown yelled, "Saw your friend Sonny and Mrs. Griffin coming down the hill."

We raced to see who could get to the ground floor first.

Books by Anna Christian

<u>Contemporary Women's fiction</u>
Then Sings My Soul
Daniel's Wife

<u>Biography</u>
Meet it, Greet it, and Defeat it! The Biography of Frances E. Williams, Actress/Activist

<u>Picture Book</u>
The Big Table, an illustrated children's book

<u>Bobby and Sonny Mysteries - Chapter Books for Preteens</u>
Mrs. Griffin is Missing and Other Stories
The Newcomer
Mr. Moore's Menagerie

Christian lives in California with her family.

Contact information: anadoodlin@yahoo.com, http://anachristian.com and http://francesplace.org.